I WANT TO READ!

Fish

Apple

Caitlin Stewart Keegan
Sian Rose Stewart Keegan
Jamie Malcolm Keegan

This Book Belongs To:

CAITLIN KEEGAN

I Want To Read!

by Betty Ren Wright

illustrated by Aliki

THIS BOOK WAS DESIGNED for boys and girls who are almost ready to read, and for those who have just discovered what fun reading can be.

READ THE STORY ALOUD to the very young child, as you would read any other picture-storybook, emphasizing how many IMPORTANT THINGS TO KNOW are found in the signs.

WITH A SLIGHTLY OLDER CHILD, read the story but give your beginning reader the satisfaction of telling you what the signs and posters say.

GOLDEN PRESS

Western Publishing Company, Inc.
Racine, Wisconsin
© MCMLXX, MCMLXV by Western Publishing Company, Inc.
All rights reserved. Produced in U.S.A.
Twelfth Golden Press Printing, 1979

ISBN 0-307-10879-1

house

boy

dog

The Story of William Tell

MY BOOK OF DOLLS

Do you know what's happened to us this year?
It's happened to me.
It's happened to Sue.

tree

It's something very special we do,
something that's fun,
something we need,
something exciting . . .

When we go to the zoo
we can find the way,
and we know what all of the signposts say.

We know what the elephant likes to eat.

This elephant likes peanuts.

We know what time the seal has his meal.

The seal has his meal at one o'clock.

We know the name of the tall giraffe

(It's a funny name.

It makes us laugh.)

The giraffe's name is Shorty.

And when we're hungry we can easily tell
what the candy-man has to sell.
We read the signs. (We really do!)

The man says, "What'll it be for you?"
"Peanuts, please," I usually say.
Or, "Popcorn, please," another day.

When we come home from school each day
we sort the letters (we know what they say!)....
Two for Daddy,
one for Mommy,
and, on our birthday, one two three
great big letters for Sue and me.

Happy
birthday
to you!

from
Tom

Have a
happy day!

Love,
Grandma

I Love
You
Aunt
Mary

When we go to the store we can find the tools.

When we play a game we can read the rules.

When the circus is coming, we know the day,

and we can help Daddy find the way.

The best thing of all—we can read our books.
We can read them ourselves.
We know what they say!

If Mommy is busy
and Daddy is busy
we can read them ourselves
any time of the day.

The little
truck
had a
secret.

"LOOK!" said the little plane.
"We are going to fly into a cloud!"

Trucks,

planes,

Happy the Horse

My name is No-No
and I am a cat.

horses,

cats,

turtles,

The giant is as tall as a tree.

giants,

this-and-thats,

Little Red Riding Hood

ABC

a big blue kite,

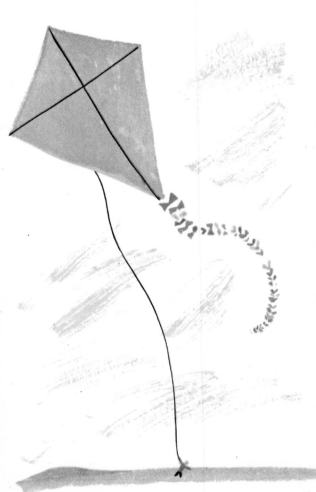

"Kite! Kite! Take me along!"
cried Tom.

Jack looked up at the
tall beanstalk.

a magic seed . . .

they're all in our books,
and WE CAN READ!

Well, that's what's happened to us this year.
It's happened to me.
It's happened to Sue.
And one thing I'm certain is
true, true TRUE!
You're going to be glad when it happens to you!

Bird

Flower

Cinderella

Bunny

Miss Pink

They lived happily
ever after.

Age 9

Age 5